P9-DNB-870

With thanks to the Preschool Camp and the Learning Center at the Claudio Marzollo Community Center of Philipstown, N.Y.
— J.M.

With thanks to Polly Townsend and the Desmond-Fish Library's Parent / Child Workshop
— W.W.

No part of this publication may be reproduced, stored in a retrieval system, or transmitted in any form or by any means, electronic, mechanical, photocopying, recording, or otherwise, without written permission of the publisher. For information regarding permission, write to Scholastic Inc., Attention: Permissions Department, 557 Broadway, New York, NY 10012.

ISBN 978-0-545-41583-5

I Spy Animals was originally published as a board book under the title *I Spy Little Animals*.

Text copyright © 1998 by Jean Marzollo.
"Creepy Crawly Cave," "Mirror Maze," "Prizes to Win," and "Puppet Theater" from *I Spy Fun House* © 1993 by Walter Wick; "Chain Reaction," "The Hidden Clue," "The Mysterious Monster," and "The Toy Box Solution" from *I Spy Mystery* © 1993 by Walter Wick; "Clouds," "The Deep Blue Sea," and "Yikes!" from *I Spy Fantasy* © 1994 by Walter Wick; "Storybook Theater" from *I Spy School Days* © 1995 by Walter Wick.
All Published by Scholastic Inc.

All rights reserved. Published by Scholastic Inc.
SCHOLASTIC, CARTWHEEL BOOKS, and associated logos are trademarks and/or registered trademarks of Scholastic Inc.

10 9 8 7 13 14 15 16

Printed in the U.S.A. 40 • This edition first printing, January 2012

I SPY ANIMALS

Rhymes by Jean Marzollo

Photographs by Walter Wick

SCHOLASTIC INC.
New York Toronto London Auckland
Sydney Mexico City New Delhi Hong Kong

I spy

a bird

and a small balloon.

I spy

a turtle

and a little spoon.

FINISH

I spy
a horse
and a yellow duck.

I spy

an elephant

and a zebra truck.

I spy

a bike

and a dog with a hat.

I spy

a fire hydrant

and a kitty cat.

R
R
A
9
1
3
MAYFLOWER
FOX
K

I spy

a horse

and a little red car.

HORSE

I spy

a door

and a starfish star.

I spy

a fish

and a yellow dog.

I

I spy

a mouse

and a spotted frog.

I spy

a duck,

a phone,

a tree.

STOP

I spy

a bunny rabbit

just for me!

When you are done,
go back and look…

rabbit

two fish

panda with a ball

What else can you find in your I Spy book?

leopard

lizard

lamb

Collect the I Spy books

Classics

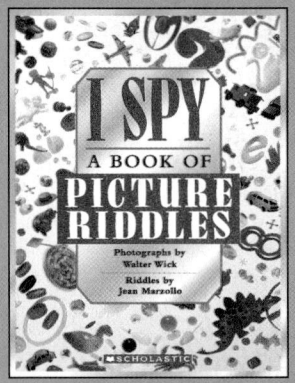

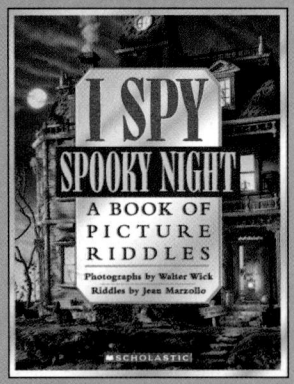

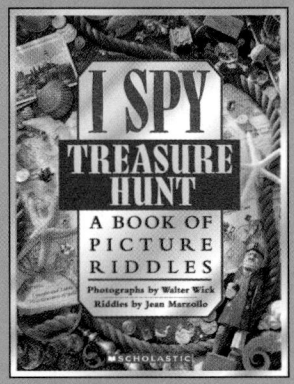

Collect the I Spy books

Challengers

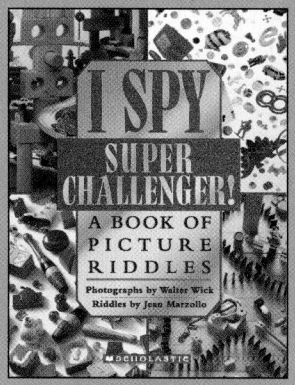

Also available are *I Spy A to Z*, *I Spy Spectacular*, I Spy early readers, I Spy Little board books, and *I Spy Phonics Fun*.

Find all the I Spy books and more at www.scholastic.com/ispy/.